BLITZ BABY

THERESA TOMLINSON
ILLUSTRATED BY SUSIE JENKIN-PEARCE

ORCHARD BOOKS

Chapter 1
SLEEPING ON THE SETTEE

"Sleep downstairs on the settee? Not on Christmas Eve!" Jamie didn't like the idea at all. "It'll spoil everything," he said.

On Christmas morning he'd always woken early in his own bed, before any sign of daylight. He'd stretch out his toes, feeling for the weight of presents at the bottom of the bed, and listen for the crackle of wrapping paper. After a moment or two of lying there blissfully, he'd sit up and slowly open each present one at a time, a big, daft grin on his face.

But this year wouldn't be the same at all, because Grandad Jim was coming to stay. Jim had worked all his life in one of the Sheffield steelworks and now he'd got a bad back, so he couldn't possibly sleep on the settee. Grandad would have to sleep in Jamie's bed, and Jamie was going to have to sleep downstairs in the front room instead.

"It's just for this year," his mother told him. "In the spring we're going to move into a bigger house, one with three bedrooms."

Jamie sighed at the thought of that; it didn't make him feel any better. He didn't want to move house, he liked things the way they were. Why should anything have to change?

"It'll be fun sleeping downstairs," his mother insisted. "You'll be able to stay up late with us and I'll bring a duvet and pillow down for you, then you'll wake in the morning with the Christmas tree right there beside you. Your presents will arrive just the same – don't worry about that!"

Jamie wasn't convinced. Christmas Eve was the one night of all the year when he actually didn't mind going to bed.

In past years, Grandma and Grandad Jim had come round for Christmas dinner, but they never stayed the night. This year had to be different because Grandma had died last Spring and Jim had been very quiet and lost without her.

"Couldn't he just come for dinner, like last year?" Jamie tried hopefully. After all, Jim only lived three streets away.

"I'm not having my dad wake up on Christmas morning all alone, in an empty house," Mum said, her eyes going all watery. "He's got to come and stay here, and that's that."

Jamie could see that there would be no point in arguing with her anymore.

"It's all very well for her," he muttered to himself. "She doesn't have to give her room up for him!"

"Hey, mate," Dad caught hold of Jamie and whispered in his ear. "Jim's very sad at the moment. Let's try to be kind to him. Remember we called you James, after your grandad. He's very fond of you, you know."

"'Suppose so!" Jamie agreed.

The days leading up to Christmas passed in a blur of excitement. There were parties, the school play, going into town to look at the lights and decorating the tree. When Christmas Eve did at last arrive, Grandad came round with a little bag and Jamie watched as he unpacked his pyjamas and toothbrush in his bedroom.

9

"Now then, lad, I've brought something special for your tree," Jim said, handing Jamie a tiny parcel wrapped in tissue paper.

Jamie smiled as he opened it, hoping for more chocolate money, but when he saw what it was, it was really difficult to keep that polite smile there on his face. Out of the tissue paper slipped a small, grubby, pink shape with a worn thread of cotton attached through a hole in the top.

"Doesn't look much, I know," Grandad smiled and put out a rather shaky finger to touch it. "It's the Blitz Baby tree decoration," he said. "That's what we always called it. I made it during the war, when I was about your age – made it out of dough, just before we got bombed. It's amazing that it's lasted so long. We always said that it must be lucky. You go and hang it on your tree."

Obediently, Jamie carried it downstairs, but he looked down at the Blitz Baby with disgust. He wasn't having that thing on his shiny, bright Christmas tree, with its flashing lights and sparkling tinsel. The Blitz Baby looked very old and had lost one of its legs. It had once been painted pink all over, but now most of the paint had flaked off, leaving the ancient, grizzled greyness of the dough showing through.

"Oh, the Blitz Baby." His mother saw it in his hands and pounced on it. "Fancy my dad bringing that. It always had pride of place on our Christmas tree when I was a girl."

And before Jamie could stop her, she was hanging it up on their Christmas tree, right in the front and high up, just beneath the fairy with her star-tipped wand and silver pearly wings.

Jamie pulled a face. "Looks stupid," he said.

But his father gave him a sharp warning look that made him shrug his shoulders and say no more.

Jamie did find that he enjoyed the evening. For once he ate and drank as much as he wanted and nobody told him to stop. There were crisps, mince pies, lemonade and chocolate biscuits. The grown-ups drank sherry and became very jolly, though Jamie did notice that just now and again his grandfather would go quiet for a moment and sigh deeply. He could see that his dad had been right. Underneath all the smiles and jokes, Grandad Jim was still sad.

Chapter 2
TOMORROW YOU CAN GO IN THE BIN

When at last all the grown-ups had gone off to bed, Jamie tried to settle down on the settee with his head on a pillow and a warm duvet over him. It wasn't easy, even though Mum had put out the flashing tree lights, in case they kept him awake. From a little gleam of light that crept in from the hallway, he could still see the ornaments twinkling gently. He remembered that the Blitz

Baby was there, just beneath the fairy in a dark spot.

"Huh! I'm not going to sleep with that thing messing up my tree!" he murmured.

So he got out of bed, and crept over to the tree, reaching high up into the spiky, pine-scented branches. He grabbed the Blitz Baby and unhooked it, then stood back. "That's better!"

Now he could get to sleep properly. He returned to the settee and settled down, with the thing still in his hand. He didn't know what else to do with it, so he thrust it under his pillow. "Tomorrow you can go in the bin," he promised. Then, at last, he closed his eyes and drifted off to sleep.

Jamie woke with a jump. A terrible noise had disturbed him. It was a wailing sound that steadily got higher and louder. He clapped his hands over his ears, but the wail grew louder still, then suddenly stopped. He sat up on the settee. That horrible noise had made his heart start to thunder like a drum. He couldn't think straight at all. What on earth was going on? He was in pitch darkness now, even the faint light coming from the hallway had gone. Had there been an electricity cut?

"Mum!" he shouted.

"Get down into the cellar," a woman's voice answered him, but it didn't sound like his mother.

"Come on, James," the same voice shouted again. "It's happened love. It's the *Luftwaffe*. Everyone said it would happen and it has."

Jamie's heart pounded now. None of this made sense. "I can't see anything," he shouted again. He could hear the clatter of footsteps on wood, as though lots of people were running down an uncarpeted staircase, then at last came the faint glimmer of candlelight.

Somebody came into the room, carrying a candle stuck inside a small lantern. They grabbed hold of his hand in the dark and pulled him along with them. Jamie was deeply shocked, but he had no choice but to go.

He seemed to be with a lot of other children all crushing together, pushing and shoving, as they went down some stairs into a cellar. "I must be dreaming," Jamie muttered. "Our house doesn't have a cellar."

This wasn't his house, he wasn't even with his own family. It was completely mad.

The woman who'd got hold of his hand pushed him in front of her, onto the lower level of a roughly built, wooden bunk bed. The bunks fitted tightly into a tiny, brick-built room, set right inside the cellar. "Harry, you go there with James," she ordered. "Then you David, Lizzy on the top."

Jamie saw that the woman was very fat and wearing a loose, flowered dress underneath a big brown overcoat.

Two more bodies scrambled onto the lower bunk beside him, so that he was wedged into a corner, with Harry's elbow sticking into him. A girl, who must be Lizzie, scrambled up onto the bunk above them.

"I'm just going to fetch Madge," the woman told them.

They were suddenly left in pitch darkness again as she hurried back up the cellar stairs. Jamie couldn't see a thing, not even his hand when he held it up in front of his face.

"Oh, why do we have to have Madge?" the one who was called Harry moaned. "I bet she brings her canary again."

"Shut up moaning!" Lizzie spoke sharply above them. Then she giggled and whispered, "Click! Click! Click!"

"You shut up!" David gave an answering giggle.

Sure enough, as the faint candle lantern lit the cellar once again, they saw the dark shadow of the woman who'd held Jamie's hand coming down the stairs, and with her another much older woman, who wore an overcoat with another jacket on top of it, and a rather smart, velvet hat on her head. She stumbled a little in the shadows at the bottom of the steps.

"They're saying it's a purple alert," the old woman said, her voice all shaky. "Oh dear, Annie, that's serious isn't it?"

Jamie saw that she managed to clutch a birdcage tightly in her hands, complete with twittering canary inside.

"Yes. I'm afraid this is it, Madge. They're really coming

to get Sheffield tonight. We always knew they'd come for the steelworks!"

"Don't like this!" Madge muttered. "I'm best under my own bed. They wouldn't get me there!"

"No, Madge, this is much better," Annie insisted. "They won't get you here in our strong, little shelter that Fred has built."

Jamie opened his mouth to ask who it was that was coming to get them, but the words never came out, for a very frightening thought had come to him. Somehow, at the back of his mind, he knew who it was that was coming to get them. He'd seen pictures on the television of people sheltering together in a small space like this, and he'd heard that word before – the *Luftwaffe*. It was bombs that they were afraid of and the *Luftwaffe* were the

German air force. Somehow he seemed to be stuck here with these strangers in the middle of the Second World War.

Chapter 3
SKINNY JIM

Jamie shuddered. If this was a dream, it was a very real and scary one. Were bombs really coming? He seemed to remember that his grandad sometimes talked about being bombed, but Jamie had never really listened properly.

"What about Dad?" Harry whispered beside him, his chin trembling.

The woman shrugged her shoulders.

"Your dad's driving back to Sheffield tonight with a lorry full of steel girders," she said briskly. "He'll take shelter somehow, I'm sure."

But the worried look on her face told them that she wasn't sure at all.

The two women settled down on stools, so close that Jamie could have put out his hand to touch them. They were all cramped together and Madge started clicking her false teeth in a nervous kind of way, that made Jamie understand why the other children didn't want her there.

It was only now that Jamie got the chance to look at everyone properly. All the children seemed to be wearing old-fashioned dressing gowns over their night clothes. He looked down to see that he, himself, wore faded, red-striped pyjamas, beneath a worn dressing gown. The two other boys, who were both older than him, seemed somehow familiar, but he couldn't think why, they weren't friends of his.

Then he noticed that though Annie had a fat stomach, the rest of her was quite thin. He knew at once what it meant. He'd seen it before when his next-door neighbour had got fat in just the same way. "You're having a baby," he couldn't help but say it.

David and Harry both giggled. "He's just noticed," they nudged him.

Lizzy's head appeared upside down from the top bunk, her long hair swinging about so that she looked very strange.

"Skinny Jim," she said. "He's a bit dim, is Skinny Jim!"

But Annie smiled kindly at Jamie and bent forward to touch his knee. "It'll be a new brother or sister for you, James," she said.

Jamie was so shocked that he couldn't speak.

Though he was astonished by what the woman had said, there was no time to try to understand, for in the distance they began to hear some really frightening sounds that made his back feel cold and shivery. It started gently, a distant buzz, as though bees were swarming overhead, followed by small bangs like a firecracker. The buzzing grew louder and turned into a grating drone, then a great swooping roar. An ear-splitting crack, like thunder, followed, as the droning faded away into the distance.

Though it was quite cold in the cellar, Jamie found that his forehead was wet with sweat. Lizzy started to whimper up on the top bunk. "My dad, my dad," she wailed.

"What about us," said Harry in a small voice. "I think it's us they're coming to get."

"Right above us, damn them," David said, fiercely, though his voice wobbled a bit.

"No, they're not," his mother told him firmly, pressing her lips together. "It only sounds like that. I'm sure they're really miles away."

There were a few moments silence, but then the terrifying sounds started again. They came back again and again, so that it was hard to know how long it was that they'd been squeezed together in the cellar. Harry snuggled close, clutching tightly onto Jamie's arm at the sound of a particularly close crack and bang. Harry's hair smelled of disinfectant and though it was strange having somebody you didn't really know clutching onto you like that, the feeling of warmth that came from the small hand was comforting in this frightening place.

Annie shuffled about and rubbed her back while Madge clicked her teeth.

"Are you all right, Mam?" Lizzie's worried voice came from above.

"Yes, yes," Annie shrugged. "It's just a bit of a stomach-ache. It's rushing up and down those stairs that's caused it, I expect."

Nobody spoke for a while in the cramped shelter. All they could hear was the click of Madge's teeth and the twittering of her canary. Then, suddenly, Annie gave a muffled cry.

"Mam," said Lizzie in a frightened

"Up onto the top bunk! Up you get, all you lads!"

They didn't hesitate to obey. All three boys scrambled at once onto the top bunk beside Lizzy, who quickly moved up to make room for them.

"Now then, Annie, you get yourself onto this bottom bunk."

"But Madge." Annie's voice sounded very weak and worried now. "I do need a midwife, I think."

"Well, you've got one, my darling," was the surprising reply. "Didn't you know that I was a midwife? It's years since I've practised, of course, but don't you fret. I can remember everything that's important."

"Oh dear! Oh Madge!" Annie was too flustered to argue; she did as she was told and struggled onto the lower bunk bed.

"Now," said Madge. "I shall be needing string, clean towels and scissors. You'll have to go up and find them for me, Lizzie. Can you do it?"

"Yes," Lizzie said, and at once she climbed down from the top bunk and set off bravely up the cellar stairs, taking the candle with her.

Chapter 4
AN IMPORTANT JOB TO DO

They were plunged into complete darkness again, while bombs seemed to crash down on them from above. Annie grunted and moaned, but Madge's voice was strong and reassuring. "That's it, darling. This baby is fine, it's a strong little thing. I can feel its little legs kicking and its arms punching away." Then, suddenly, there was another sound that filled the tiny shelter, a strong wailing bellow.

"Is it born?" Harry asked in a frightened voice.

"Yes, it is," Madge told them.

Just then, the flicker of the candle returned, and Lizzie came back down the cellar steps, with her arms full of towels.

"Oh Madge," she cried. "You are a real midwife. It's a girl. We've got a sister."

"Now look here, dear, have you got everything?" Madge was concerned with practical things.

"Yes." Lizzie was close to tears.

"Jolly good – now you get quickly up onto that bunk again. There's an important job for you all to do. Get a clean towel ready!"

As soon as Lizzie had climbed back beside them, they made a small space in the middle of the bunk and spread out a clean but rather ragged towel. Then, after a moment or two, Madge struggled up from the floor where she'd been kneeling and reached up to them, plopping an angry, little red-faced baby onto the towel.

"Now, this is your job," she said. "You keep your little sister warm, while I see to her mother."

They all looked at the naked baby, amazed. She howled loudly and kicked and punched with her tiny arms and legs. Then, suddenly, Jamie saw what to do. He started to unbutton his striped pyjama jacket.

"Wrap her up in our 'jamas," he said.

"Yes," said David. "That's it," and he and Harry copied.

They were rather cold for a short while, but once they'd got their dressing gowns back on, it didn't seem to matter that their chests were bare. Jamie carefully tucked his jacket, still warm from his own body, around the baby's chest. Harry covered the legs, and David slipped his jacket underneath the baby's head, wrapping it round like a shawl.

"Hush! Hush! Hush!" Lizzie crooned.

Jamie put out his hand to gently stroke the little pink cheek. The baby stopped crying at once and opened her eyes very wide, looking at them as though she'd just noticed that they were there.

"That's better," said Lizzie. "You must be good with babies, Skinny Jim."

Then, the baby thrust her tiny thumb into her mouth and started sucking very loudly and contentedly, while she continued to stare at them, as though she was very surprised to be there, but not displeased.

They all giggled. Jamie's eyes started to water and the most incredible feeling of warmth and happiness spread through him. This was the most amazing dream that he'd ever had.

"Listen," said Lizzie.

"What?" David asked, as they all went quiet.

They could hear nothing but the baby sucking her thumb, and the faint twittering of the canary. Then, suddenly, there came the great wail of the siren again, and though it made them all jump, they laughed.

"That's the 'All Clear!' They've gone!" Lizzie whispered.

The air raid was over.

The sound of footsteps coming down the cellar steps made them all look up.

"Dad! Dad you're safe," Lizzie cried.

"Is everything all right?" a tall man asked, stooping a little as he came into the shelter. His hair was powdered with dust and he looked very worried.

"Yes," said Madge, smiling at him and looking pleased with herself. "Everything is absolutely fine."

"Oh Fred! We've got a little girl," Annie told him, her voice strong and happy now. "We're going to call her after Madge. I insist upon it!"

It took quite a long time for them all to get up the cellar stairs again and when they did, there were more shocks in store for Jamie. They were in a little house that was rather like the one that he lived in, but everything was very worn and faded looking. Fred quickly drew up black blinds to let bright daylight in, but Jamie saw at once that the windows had been pasted with a criss-cross pattern of brown paper strips, so that you couldn't see out properly. A small Christmas tree stood there in the front room, but it had no decorations on it at all.

It was only when Annie at last sat down at the kitchen table, with the new baby in her arms, that she asked her husband the question that had been on all their minds. "What has happened to Sheffield?"

Fred shook his head. "Dreadful," he said. "The centre of town's gone. Cinemas, shops, that huge hotel – Marples – all rubble. Even the football ground is smashed."

Everyone stood there, quietly looking at him and feeling terrible.

"There's folk rushing about in circles," he went on. "Then there's others wandering lost, so many hurt... there must be a lot of people killed."

"Did they get the steelworks?" Harry asked.

"Yes, lad, I think they did."

Jamie began to think that it was time he woke up from this dream. It had become so uncomfortably real, he wasn't sure that it was a dream after all. Was he going to wake up? Or was he going to be stuck here forever in the middle of the war?

Nobody seemed to know what to do, but Madge took charge again. "Well, my house is still standing," she said, looking out of the window. "I'll take these children round there, so that you two can get this baby sorted out."

Chapter 5

A HANDFUL OF FLOUR

So because there seemed to be no choice about it, Jamie followed the others into Madge's house. "Right," said Madge. "I'll put the kettle on and then we'll find something to do to cheer ourselves up."

Lizzie looked very sad. "It's going to be an awful Christmas," she said.

"No, it isn't," said Madge, quite firmly. "That's what we'll do – we'll prepare for Christmas. I'll make a pudding and you can make decorations for that tree of yours."

Madge produced a roll of bright red crepe paper and some scissors. She used a bit of flour and water to mix a sticky paste and Jamie watched as the older children began making paper chains. They carefully cut short strips

of red paper, then stuck the tips together to make circles. They threaded another strip through, and stuck the ends together again, so that it wasn't long before red paper chains began to grow from their busy hands. They were soon laughing and joking together, as though everything was all right.

Madge stirred flour and an egg into her bowl, then she added a tablespoon of treacle and a few more spoonfuls of sugar, measuring everything out very carefully. Jamie watched them working cheerfully around him, and began to feel lost and lonely. What was he doing there?

He just stood there, all forlorn, until Madge looked at him over the rim of her glasses. She put her mixing bowl down and tipped a tiny amount of flour into a small china

cup. She added a bit of salt and a few drops of water from the tap, then she put her fingers in amongst it all and kneaded the mixture thoroughly.

"Here," she said. "Here's something special for young Jim to make." And she dropped the smallest ball of dough into Jamie's hand. "You make a little dough ornament," she said. "I can spare a handful of flour for such a good cause. You could make it into a snowman or a Santa Claus, or an angel with wings, then I'll cook it with the pudding and you can paint it.

Jamie could see from the way that the others looked at him that being given that small ball of dough was a real treat.

"Well, Skinny Jim, what are you going to make?" Lizzie asked.

Jamie knew what he had to do. He felt as though his life was going round in circles. It was really weird, but he just had to do it. "I'm going to make a dough baby," he said. "I'm going to paint it pink."

Harry and David burst out laughing, but Lizzie said "Ah!" and she came and gave him a gentle, little kiss on the cheek.

As she kissed him, a sort of light switch turned on in Jamie's head. His mother had told him that he'd once had an Auntie Lizzie, a great aunt who'd died when he was very small. He couldn't ever remember seeing her, the only aunt he'd got now was that chatterbox, Aunt Maggie...

He looked across Madge's scrubbed wooden table at the other two boys, who were pinching little bits of each other's crepe paper and laughing like hyenas.

He'd still got an Uncle Harry and he'd got an Uncle David too, they were Grandad's brothers. Suddenly he understood. It was almost unbelievable, but he was quite sure about it now. Those boys were his uncles and he had somehow turned into his grandfather, Jim. He was seeing through Jim's eyes and he was magically seeing things that had happened an awful long time ago. It was a crazy thought, but it made him smile – he wasn't really with strangers after all. He was with his own family!

It had all started with that dough baby, and here he was about to make it. His hands started to shake, but he felt that he had to do it. First, he squeezed the dough almost in the middle so that it made a fat, round stomach and a smaller bulge for the head. Then, he pulled out two shapes at the side for arms, and another two shapes from the lower bit for legs. The little figure, now familiar to him, grew beneath his fingers, until it was all there. It looked a bit like a gingerbread man. Madge made a small hole in the top of the doughy shape with a darning needle, then she popped it into her oven with the pudding.

It cooked hard quite quickly and while it was cooling, she gave them all some vegetable soup. Jamie found it very tasteless and watery, but he was polite and ate it all up, as he was getting rather hungry.

After they'd done the washing-up, Madge got out some little pots of paint and put newspaper on the kitchen table, so that Jamie could paint the dough baby.

He looked at the pots. "But – I need pink," he said.

"Oh dear!" Madge shook her head. "I've got white and blue and green and yellow, but I've run out of red."

"Just paint it white and make it into a snowman," David said.

Jamie began to get

a panicky feeling inside him. "But my dough baby has got to be pink," he said.

Madge frowned, and Lizzie put her hands on her hips, looking rather annoyed. "There is a war on, you know," she said.

"I've got it," said Madge. "Don't you fret, my lad." She went into her kitchen cupboard and brought out a tiny bottle of something that looked like dark red ink. "Cochineal!" she said. "Food colouring. One tiny drop of this in some white paint will make a wonderful pink."

Jamie sighed with relief. Despite her clicking false teeth, he found that he liked Madge very much.

Later that day, they went back to Annie and Fred with their arms full of dainty paper chains, Jamie proudly carrying the newly painted and varnished Blitz Baby.

The others hung the paper chains all over the tree.

"Now," said Lizzy. "You put your baby on, high as you can, Skinny Jim."

It was as he reached up to the Christmas tree that it started to happen. Even as he stretched his hand up to the branch, he knew that something was changing. His eyes went rather blurred and everything about him seemed to shimmer and shake.

"I've got to put it on the tree," he murmured, but his eyes drooped with tiredness and he felt so very warm and lazy. His hand was as heavy as lead, and he just couldn't make it lift the tiny ornament up. Then, all at once, he found himself sitting up on the settee, back in his own front room. It was still rather dark, but somebody had been in the room because there was the Christmas tree right there in front of

him, with all its flashing lights blazing.
He could feel a heavy pile of presents
on top of his feet, and he held the worn
little Blitz Baby in his hand.

"So it was a dream," he whispered.

Jamie ignored his presents and got
straight up from the settee. He reached
up high into the branches of the tree
and hung the dough baby back in the

place of honour, just beneath the feet of the fairy.

"There you are," he whispered. "Back where you should be."

Chapter 6
A NEW BATCH

It was only then that he turned to the wonderful pile of presents. He ripped open the wrappings and pulled out computer games, DVDs, sweets, chocolates, a new fleece and gloves, a ball that played a tune as you bounced it and a Santa Claus hat with a little switch on the front that made flashing lights whizz around your head. There was a box

with tubes of paint in it, to Jamie from Grandad Jim.

Jamie grinned down at the paints, they gave him an idea.

The other presents were everything that he'd hoped for, but it wasn't them that brought this bubble of excitement into his stomach. He couldn't get the strange dream out of his mind, and he couldn't wait for Grandad

Jim to wake up and come downstairs.

He tried out some of his new DVDs, but found that he couldn't concentrate on them. Then he opened the box of paints again, and fingered each gleaming tube of colour. He knew exactly what he wanted to do and he couldn't wait any longer, so he went upstairs and knocked on his grandfather's door. "I'm getting you some breakfast," he shouted. "Do you like toast?"

"Yes, please, I certainly do," Jim replied.

"I'm putting the bread in the toaster," Jamie said. "It'll be ready in a minute."

When at last his parents came downstairs they found Jamie and Jim munching their way through a mountain of toast and marmalade.

"We're going to make some more

dough babies," Jamie said. "We're going to make them as soon as we've eaten this. You have got flour and salt, haven't you?"

His mother laughed. "Oh yes, we've got plenty of flour and salt. It's not the war, you know."

Jamie and Jim worked away together at the kitchen table, while his mother

alert. That was a serious warning, that was. It meant that we must have no lights showing at all, and that planes had been spotted, heading towards us."

"Did you go into the cellar again?" Jamie asked.

Jim laughed and shook his head. "Not that time. My dad told us all to get into the back of his lorry. We took Madge and her canary with us and we took half the people in our street as well, all crammed into the back of one lorry, and off we went. Dad drove us right out of Sheffield and up onto the moors."

"So you were safe up there!"

"Yes," said Jim sadly. "We were safe, but it was a dreadful night for Sheffield. We found a farmer who kindly opened up his barn for us to shelter in and his wife made pans full of soup which she dished out to everyone. It was bitterly cold, you see."

"Must have been scary," Jamie shuddered.

Grandad Jim put down his dough and sighed. "I went with my Dad," he said. "We left the others in the barn and we went outside for a bit and looked down from the hillside onto Sheffield."

"And – what did you see?"

"Fairyland," said Jim. "It looked like fairyland, all lights and sparks and

shooting flames, but it wasn't fairyland, it was Sheffield burning. I stood there holding my dad's hand and I cried. My dad cried too."

Jamie was silent. He hadn't meant to do it, but he'd somehow made Grandad Jim sadder than ever.

But then his grandad seemed to cheer up a little. "Well – that was the best thing my dad ever did, taking us out of Sheffield that night. When we got back in the morning we found that

our house had taken a direct hit. None of us could have survived it."

"Your whole house had gone?"

Jim shook his head. "Almost gone. The crazy thing was that the front door was still standing. No house, just a front door. Our Harry went and opened the door and there behind it was our Christmas tree. It'd fallen over, of course, but we hauled it up again. All the white dust that covered its branches looked like snow, and strangest thing of all was that there, still hanging on it, was the little Blitz Baby ornament that I'd made."

Jamie picked up the Blitz Baby again. "No wonder you think it's lucky," he said, gently stroking the crumbling leg. "I think it's lucky too, and perhaps it's a bit – well, magical. But – what happened to you all? Where did you live after your whole house had gone?"

Jim smiled and his voice was full of happy memories again. "We went to live with Madge," he said. "Her house was still standing, so she just took us in – Christmas tree and all. We stayed with her right up until the end of the war."

Jamie sighed with relief and nodded. "Thank goodness for Madge," he said.

They worked together happily until a new batch of dough babies were popped into the oven with the turkey, then put into the fridge to harden and cool.

After they'd eaten a huge dinner, they mixed up a brilliant pink paint from the new tubes and painted it onto the little figures. Later that afternoon Uncle Harry and Uncle David arrived, with Aunt Maggie. They all sat around drinking sherry and talking loudly together, delighted to find the new batch of dough babies all varnished and drying above the cooker.

"Well, that's a fine family tradition that you're keeping up," Aunt Maggie said.

She bent down and kissed Jamie's cheek. He picked up the worn, one-legged little shape that had been made so long ago and held it up to her.

"It's you," he said. "You were the real Blitz Baby."

Everyone laughed. "That's right," Aunt Maggie smiled.

"Well." Jamie's mother gave a little cough and went rather pink in the face.

"While we've got so many of the family together, there's something that we'd like to tell you."

Suddenly, the whole room went quiet and everyone looked at Jamie's mum, who seemed to be lost for words now that she'd got everyone's attention. "You tell them," she nudged her husband.

Jamie's dad smiled. "We'll be moving house in the spring," he said. "We're going to need more space. You see, Jamie," he said, turning to put his arm

about him. "You are going to have a new brother or sister."

"I hope that will be all right with you," his mother added, stooping to kiss him on the head.

The room was filled with wild shouts of congratulation, but Jamie just nodded, smiling quietly to himself. "Yes, that will be fine," he whispered. "I'm very good with babies."

**Look out for more
Green Apples
from**
ORCHARD BOOKS

GERALDINE McCAUGHREAN
Illustrated by Ross Collins

JALOPY

BY GERALDINE MCCAUGHREAN

Masher and Spug ran out of the bank, chased by ten security guards, two big dogs and the clang of alarm bells. "Quick! Into the car!" cried Masher. But Jalopy was gone.

Mrs Ethel Thomas wins a beautiful shiny red car in a competition and calls the car Jalopy. But Mrs Thomas can't drive, so the car goes nowhere until one day bank-robbers Spug and Masher steal Jalopy to be their get-away car...

An exciting and funny story by a much-loved author.

MONKEY-MAN

SANDRA GLOVER

Illustrated by Garry Parsons

MONKEY-MAN

BY SANDRA GLOVER

"It was like a yeti or giant ape covered in long black hair. With huge, mad, glinting eyes. About seven feet tall. Wearing nothing but a pair of baggy shorts."

There's a hairy, scary werewolf terrorising the neighbourhood! Max and his sister, Kerry, know the creature's real secret. But saving the day may turn out to be a closer shave than they had anticipated...

A hilarious story from an acclaimed author.

ORCHARD GREEN APPLES

HARDBACK

☐ Monkey-Man   Sandra Glover   1 84362 276 9
☐ The Ugly Great Giant Malachy Doyle   1 84362 240 8
☐ Jalopy   Geraldine McCaughrean 1 84362 266 1
☐ Sugar-Bag Baby   Susan Gates   1 84362 070 7

ALL PRICED AT £8.99

PAPERBACK

☐ Monkey-Man   Sandra Glover   1 84362 278 5
☐ The Ugly Great Giant Malachy Doyle   1 84362 241 6
☐ Jalopy   Geraldine McCaughrean 1 84362 267 X
☐ Sugar-Bag Baby   Susan Gates   1 84362 071 5

ALL PRICED AT £3.99

Orchard Green Apples are available from all good book shops,
or can be ordered direct from the publisher:
Orchard Books, PO BOX 29, Douglas IM99 1BQ
Credit card orders please telephone 01624 836000 or fax 01624 837033 or visit our
Internet site: www.wattspub.co.uk
or e-mail: bookshop@enterprise.net for details.

To order please quote title, author and ISBN
and your full name and address.
Cheques and postal orders should be made payable to 'Bookpost plc.'
Postage and packing is FREE within the UK
(overseas customers should add £1.00 per book).

Prices and availability are subject to change.